FIRST CHAPTER BOOKS

Time Runners

Written by David Hunt
and illustrated by Alex Brychta

Before reading

- Read the back cover text and page 4. How do you think the Time Runners could defeat the Virans?
- Look at page 5. In which historical period do you think this story is set?

After reading

- Which part of the story did you find most exciting, the Viran in Ancient Rome or the Viran in the Time Vault?

Book quiz

1 Who did the children think the man outside the Senate was?
   a A senator
   b Julius Caesar
   c A Viran
2 What were the chutes for?
3 Where was the Viran in Ancient Rome?

See p45 for the book quiz answers!

Before you begin ...

Biff, Chip, Kipper and friends are training to be Time Runners. They are based in the Time Vault, which exists outside time. Their mission is to travel back to the past to defeat the Virans, who are trying to destroy history and bring chaos to the future.

The Time Runners have a Zaptrap - a device to capture the Virans - and a Link, which lets them communicate with the Time Vault. Apart from that, they are on their own!

The Senate Building
Rome, 44 BC

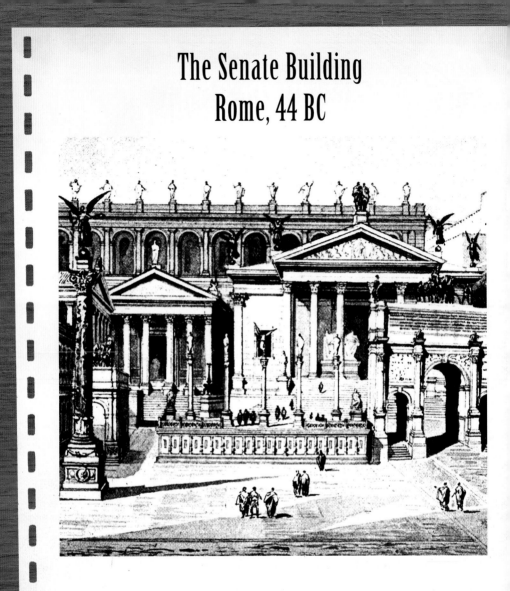

Rome didn't have a king. Instead, Roman citizens voted for two councils of leaders called the Assembly and the Senate. It was their job to discuss important issues and make laws.

Chapter 1

Chip couldn't sleep. Living in the Time Vault was exciting enough. But now they had started training to fight the Virans there was so much to learn as well.

With a sigh, he sat up and flicked a switch. The lights in his sleeping pod glowed. He picked up his training manual and began to read.

As he read, Chip held the communication Link in his hand. He couldn't wait to use it for real. He couldn't wait to become a Time Runner.

Chapter 2

The day's training began in the laboratory. "You look half asleep," said Neena as Chip shuffled in, late.

"At least he's got up," said Wilf, closing his locker. "Tyler must still be in bed!"

At that moment, the door burst open. It was Mortlock. Behind him, something zoomed into the room.

"Tyler!" everyone gasped.

"And his new techno-chair!" announced Mortlock.

Tyler turned suddenly and then skidded to a stop.

"Do you like it?" he grinned. "Mortlock built it. Now I'll be able to do anything you lot can!"

"And a lot more!" smiled Mortlock.

"Impressive!" said Nadim.

Everyone gathered around Tyler. Chip looked at the control panels on the chair. "What does this one do?" he asked, pushing one of the buttons.

"No!" yelled Tyler. But it was too late.

Tyler shot backwards and slammed into the lockers. Immediately the chair lurched forward. "Whoa!" giggled Tyler. "Stop!"

They all laughed at the sight of Tyler zipping wildly across the laboratory. But suddenly the laughing stopped. Tyler was heading straight for the vat where the captured Virans were held.

They held their breath as he ploughed into the side of the vat with a loud crash.

The glass vat shuddered. The black matter stirred, sparking and hissing angrily inside the glass chamber.

Everyone rushed to help Tyler. "Even behind the glass, those Virans are scary," Tyler said in a shaky voice.

The vat slowly settled with a quiet hiss.

Mortlock quickly checked it. "It seems all right," he said. "No harm done. But we must be careful near the vat."

Chapter 3

The training carried on all day. There was a lot to learn about the Link. As he listened, Nadim flicked up the secret lid and studied the tiny screen and keyboard.

But Tyler couldn't concentrate. He tried to listen to Mortlock, but something was bothering him. He kept thinking about the Virans and how frightening they were.

Finally Mortlock said, "So remember, with the Link you'll be able to talk to the Time Vault when you are on a mission. The Link also sends and receives text downloads." He looked around the room. "Any questions?"

Tyler put up his hand. "I'm worried. We can't use the Link to protect ourselves against Virans, can we?" he asked. "We've been lucky so far, but we won't always be."

The others agreed. "Yeah," said Nadim. "I mean, how are we supposed to trap them and bring them back?"

Mortlock nodded thoughtfully. "It's time to show you," he said. "Let's go!"

No one had noticed, but all this time the Viran vat had continued to hiss quietly . . . Something was not right.

Chapter 4

Everyone followed Mortlock into the library. At the far end, he stopped and pulled a large book away from the shelf.

Immediately the whole bookcase juddered, and then slid inwards like giant doors. Beyond the bookcase was a dark space. Mortlock stepped into the darkness. Lights blinked on to reveal a large room. The bookcase doors closed behind them.

"This is the Control Centre," said Mortlock. In the centre of the space, on a desk, was the TimeWeb. Its mass of glowing threads shimmered gently. In front of it was the Matrix and beside it was a globe that glowed with a faint light.

Mortlock pointed at the open tubes that dropped into the space. They were chutes. He explained that they were connected to the sleeping pods. "With these, you can get here in seconds," smiled Mortlock.

"So that's what the chutes are," grinned Wilma. "Cool!"

Next, Mortlock slid open a drawer in the desk. He took out a silver ball and held it up. "This is a Zaptrap," he said. "They are used to catch Virans."

Mortlock began to explain how they worked. But Chip's mind wandered. It had been a long day. Sleep – the thought of it made him yawn.

Mortlock stopped talking. He smiled at Chip. "Perhaps we should all get some rest. It's been a long day."

Mortlock began to hand out Zaptraps. "Tomorrow I'll show you how they work. For now, take them with you and get used to them. Look at the section on Zaptraps in your manuals."

Meanwhile, back in the laboratory, the Viran vat continued to hiss.

Chapter 5

Even though Chip was tired, he still couldn't sleep. So he lay in bed reading. Eventually, he fell asleep still holding the manual.

A voice jolted Chip from his deep sleep.

"Chip to Control immediately," it barked. It came from the speaker in his pod. He had overslept. He was late for training again.

Chip scrambled to the chute. He hadn't used it before. "Here goes!" he thought and he launched himself down it.

He landed with a loud thud in Control. "So glad you could join us," laughed Mortlock. But something was wrong. Chip was in pain. He had twisted his ankle.

"You'd better rest it," said Biff.

" 'Ere, Chip, I'll give you a lift back to your pod," said Tyler. "Hop on!"

Chip climbed on to the techno-chair and Tyler spun it round. But as they headed out to the library, there was a grinding sound. Smoke billowed from under the chair and it stopped suddenly.

"Oh no!" said Tyler.

Mortlock studied the techno-chair's motor. "It may take time to fix," he tutted.

"I'm sorry," said Tyler. "It must have been damaged when I crashed into the vat."

"Don't worry," smiled Mortlock. "I'll push Chip back to his pod, then I'll take the chair to my workshop and try to fix it. The rest of you stay here. Use the time to study the TimeWeb."

He pushed Chip out into the library, and the bookcase doors closed behind them.

Chapter 6

They looked at the TimeWeb in silence.
"It's like a map," Wilma suddenly said. "A giant map of history. Every point of light is a moment from the past."

"Every moment affects the next right up to the present," added Neena.

The TimeWeb stirred. A point of light suddenly turned black, sending a pulse of darkness towards the edge of the web.

They watched in horror. "Is it a Viran attack?" asked Kipper. "Now what do we do?"

Tyler tried to call Mortlock on his Link, but there was no answer.

"We have to do something!" said Biff.

Tyler peered into the globe next to the Matrix. "Ancient Rome, 44 BC. The Virans must be attacking," he gasped. "You have to go now! I'll stay on Control."

They stepped into the portal and in a few head-spinning seconds they had arrived.

Within a moment, Tyler had contacted them on the Link. "What can you see?"

Wilma whispered into her Link. "Early morning. A quiet street. Tall buildings like blocks of flats. A large marble building with tall columns covered in scaffolding."

"Looks like it's being rebuilt," added Biff.

Tyler had done some research in the library. "It's the Senate building," he said. "In 44 BC the Senate was closed for repairs."

"What's the Senate?" asked Kipper.

"It's where the Roman government – the senators – met," said Tyler. He quickly looked in a book. "Oh no!"

"What is it?" asked Neena.

"44 BC is when the leader, Julius Caesar, was assassinated by some of the senators."

At that moment, a man turned into the street and walked quickly toward the Senate.

"Wait!" whispered Nadim. "He looks important. He's wearing a ... um," he hesitated.

"A toga!" interrupted Wilf. "We did this at school."

"He could be Julius Caesar!" gasped Kipper.

"Possibly," said Tyler. "But it is more likely that he might be a senator."

Suddenly, from the shadows, a rough man leapt forward and dashed after the senator.

"He's going to attack him," gasped Biff. "Supposing he's a Viran? What if that man *is* Julius Caesar? I'll use my Zaptrap!"

"Wait!" said Tyler. "You have to be sure it's a Viran. You must not get involved otherwise. Just wait!"

Chapter 7

Chip woke with a start. Over the pod's speaker he could hear Floppy barking.

He hobbled down the slope to level one. It sounded as if Floppy was in the library. Why hadn't the others heard him?

As he pulled open the library door, his blood froze. He saw a swirling mass of darkness. It was ripping the library to pieces. It could only be a Viran. It must have escaped from the vat in the laboratory.

Meanwhile, back in Ancient Rome ...

"We must stop him," said Neena. "Before it's too late."

The rough man caught up with the senator, and grabbed hold of him.

"He has to be a Viran," cried Biff. She held up her Zaptrap. "Tyler ... answer me! I'm going to launch it."

"But we have to be sure," gasped Wilf.

Biff held her breath. "I've got one chance," she thought.

At the same time, in the Time Vault ...

As fast as he could, Chip limped back
up to his pod. He had to think quickly. He
spoke into his Link. "Is anyone there?"

Tyler answered. "Chip? I'm at Control.
We've had an emergency and ..."

Chip interrupted him. "There's a Viran
in the library. It must be trying to get into
Control. Are you all safe? Can the Viran get
to you?"

Tyler was scared. He had locked the bookcase doors, but on the other side he could hear crashing sounds. If the Viran got in, they were finished. The Viran would destroy the TimeWeb. From the library came a loud thud. The bookcase doors shook.

Tyler spoke to Chip urgently. "I can't move quickly without my chair. The others are out in the TimeWeb. I don't know where Mortlock is."

"Call them back," yelled Chip. "Now!"

Just as Biff was about to throw her Zaptrap, the rough man pulled the senator backwards. From the roof of the senate, a huge block of stone crashed to the street where the senator had been, a second earlier.

The man had saved the senator's life. Biff and the others had got it wrong. Nadim looked up at the roof. A shadowy figure stared back. "Viran!" Nadim shouted.

Biff threw her Zaptrap.

Everyone's Link buzzed. It was Tyler. "Emergency! Get back, now!" he said.

Chapter 8

Chip could hear the crashing below his pod. It was getting louder and more frantic. He hadn't been able to contact Mortlock either. Suddenly Tyler's voice burst from Chip's Link. "I've called them back! But maybe it's too late. I think the Viran's about to break through. Oh no, it's ..." Then silence.

Chip clasped his Zaptrap. "I've got one chance!" he thought, and he threw himself down the chute.

He hit the ground hard. His bad leg buckled under him. Out of the corner of his eye, he glimpsed the Viran.

He launched his Zaptrap as he fell. As it flew, it opened up and released a bolt of plasma. Instantly the Viran froze. It was sucked into the trap which snapped shut.

"You're history!" Chip screamed.

Chip had fainted with pain. He came round and saw everyone looking down at him.

Mortlock held Chip's Zaptrap which had trapped the Viran. He smiled gently. "I'm sorry I wasn't there for you," he said. "But I had to deal with the vat. It must have been damaged by Tyler's chair. There were other Virans trying to escape from it."

Mortlock took Biff's Zaptrap. "But you dealt with it. Well done! You've just proved you are ready to be Time Runners."

Tyler's Mission Report

Location:	Date:
Ancient Rome	15th March 44BC
Mission Status:	Viran Status:
Open and unfinished.	Biff and Chip zapped 2 Virans.

Notes: Time Runner training completed.

One of the hardest things to learn is how to judge a situation. Things can look very different depending on your point of view. The way you see something might not be the only way to look at it.

Good job Biff didn't throw her Zaptrap at the man she thought was attacking the Senator. She hadn't seen that he was actually trying to save the Senator.

The trick is not to make up your mind too quickly. Always try to see things from as many points of view as possible.

Sign off: ....Tyler............................

History: downloaded!
Rome

Rome was a place, but it was also an idea.
It was not only Rome itself that grew from a few villages
to a magnificent city. The idea of Rome – the Roman
way of life – spread out to the furthest points of the
known world.

Though these places would become 'Roman', they were
not Rome. There was only one Rome and for many
centuries it was the capital of the world. So in order to
rule, Rome had to keep a very powerful army.

Yet, the strange thing is, for many centuries, Rome had no overall leader. So who made all the decisions?

It was the people themselves. Romans voted for their leaders – called the Assembly and the Senate.

The idea that the people were in charge was very important to the Romans. So when an army leader called Julius Caesar became too powerful, the Senate became worried. They decided that the only way to stop Caesar was to assassinate him.

Julius Caesar

So on March 15th 44 BC, more than sixty senators waited for Caesar at the Senate with daggers hidden beneath their togas, ready to kill him.

For more information, see the Time Chronicles website: **www.oxfordprimary.co.uk/timechronicles**

Glossary

assassinated *(page 27)* Murdered or killed. *44 BC is when the leader, Julius Caesar, was assassinated by some of the Senators.*

Caesar *(page 27)* Julius Caesar was a Roman General. Years later, when Rome was ruled by one leader, they were always given the title 'Caesar'.

chutes *(page 17)* Large tubes or tunnels used to slide down. *"So that's what the chutes are," grinned Wilma.*

frantic *(page 35)* Excited, wild, out of control. *It was getting louder and more frantic.*

ploughed *(page 11)* Here means 'moved forward in a clumsy way'. *... he ploughed into the side of the vat with a loud crash.*

Senate *(page 27)* Ancient Roman community leaders who discussed important issues and made laws. The word is also used for the building where they met. *In 44 BC the Senate was closed for repairs.*

toga *(page 27)* A long length of cloth wrapped around the body. Only Roman citizens were allowed to wear them. *"A toga!" interrupted Wilf. "We did this at school."*

Thesaurus: Another word for ...
frantic *(page 35)* ferocious, fierce, savage.

Have you read them all yet?

Level 11:

Level 12:

Time Runners	Mission Victory
Tyler: His Story	The Enigma Plot
A Jack and Three Queens	The Thief Who Stole Nothing

More great fiction from Oxford Children's:

www.winnie-the-witch.com

www.dinosaurcove.co.uk

About the Authors

Roderick Hunt MBE - creator of best-loved characters Biff, Chip, Kipper, Floppy and their friends. His first published stories were those he told his two sons at bedtime. Rod lives in Oxfordshire, in a house not unlike the house in the Magic Key adventures. In 2008, Roderick received an MBE for services to education, particularly literacy.

Roderick Hunt's son **David Hunt** was brought up on his father's stories and knows the world of Biff, Chip and Kipper intimately. His love of history and a good story has sparked many new ideas, resulting in the *Time Chronicles* series. David has had a successful career in the theatre, most recently working on scripts for Jude Law's *Hamlet* and *Henry V,* as well as Derek Jacobi's *Twelfth Night.*

Joint creator of the best-loved characters Biff, Chip, Kipper, Floppy and their friends, **Alex Brychta MBE** has brought each one to life with his fabulous illustrations, which are known and loved in many schools today. Following the Russian occupation of Czechoslovakia, Alex Brychta moved with his family from Prague to London. He studied graphic design and animation, before moving to the USA where he worked on animation for Sesame Street. Since then he has devoted many years of his career to *Oxford Reading Tree,* bringing detail, magic and humour to every story! In 2012 Alex received an MBE for services to children's literature.

Roderick Hunt and Alex Brychta won the prestigious Outstanding Achievement Award at the Education Resources Awards in 2009.

43

Levelling info for parents

What do the levels mean?

Read with Biff Chip & Kipper First Chapter Books have been designed by educational experts to help children develop as readers.

Each book is carefully levelled to allow children to make gradual progress and to feel confident and enjoy reading.

The Oxford Levels you will see on these books are used by teachers and are based on years of research in schools. Below is a summary of what each Oxford Level means, so that you can help your child to improve and enjoy their reading.

The books at Level 11 (Brown Book Band):

At this level, the sentence structures are becoming longer and more complex. The story plot may be more involved and there is a wider vocabulary. However, the proportion of unknown words used per paragraph/page is still carefully controlled to help build their reading stamina and allow children to read independently.

This level mostly covers characterisation through characters' actions and words rather than through description. The story may be organised in various ways, e.g. chronologically, thematically, sequentially, as relevant to the text type and subject.

The books at Level 12 (Grey Book Band):

At this level, the sentences are becoming more varied in structure and length. Though still straightforward, more inference may be required, e.g. in dialogue to work out who is speaking. Again, the story may be organised in various ways: chronologically, thematically, sequentially, etc., so that children can reflect on how the organisation helps the reader to understand the text.

The *Times Chronicles* books are also ideal for older children who feel less confident and need more practice in order to build stamina. The text is written to be age and ability appropriate, but also engaging, motivating and funny, making them a pleasure for children to read at this stage of their reading development.

OXFORD
UNIVERSITY PRESS

Great Clarendon Street, Oxford, OX2 6DP,
United Kingdom

Oxford University Press is a department of the University of Oxford.
It furthers the University's objective of excellence in research, scholarship,
and education by publishing worldwide. Oxford is a registered trade mark
of Oxford University Press in the UK and in certain other countries

Text © Roderick Hunt and David Hunt

Text written by David Hunt, based on the original characters
created by Roderick Hunt and Alex Brychta

Illustrations © Alex Brychta

The moral rights of the authors have been asserted

Database rights Oxford University Press (maker)

First published 2010
This edition published in 2015

British Library Cataloguing in Publication Data
Data available

978-0-19-273911-7

1 3 5 7 9 10 8 6 4 2

Paper used in the production of this book is a natural, recyclable product
made from wood grown in sustainable forests. The manufacturing process
conforms to the environmental regulations of the country of origin.

Printed in China

Acknowledgements: The publisher and authors would like to thank the following for
their permission to reproduce photographs and other copyright material:

P3 Iguasu/Shutterstock; **P3ml** Leigh Prather/Shutterstock; **P4tl** Blaz Kure/Shutterstock;
P4tr Ragnarock/Shutterstock; **P4ml** INTERFOTO/Alamy; **P37** Ragnarock/Shutterstock; **P38** Valentin
Agapov; **P38tl** Hisom Sliviu/Shutterstock; **P38ml** magicinfoto/Shutterstock; **P38bl** c./Shutterstock;
P39 Ragnarock/Shutterstock; **P39tl** Maugli/Shutterstock; **P39ml** World History Archive/Alamy; **P39bl**
Mary Evans Picture Library/Alamy; **P38-39** Blaz Kure/Shutterstock; **P38-39** Jakub Krechowicz; **P38-39**
Picsfive/Shutterstock; **P40** Blaz Kure/Shutterstock.

Book quiz answers
1 b
2 To get to the Control Centre quickly.
3 On the roof.